Solve It Yourself

Mysteries for Midnight

Written by Carol Beach York
Illustrated by John Lawn

Watermill Press

ISBN 0-89375-695-4

Contents

Midnight is an hour when strange and mysterious things can happen. Midnight is a good time to be safely home in bed. But even then, things can happen—as you'll see in the stories that follow.

Read these stories carefully. Each one offers a baffling case. But if you're a good detective, you'll be able to unravel the clues that will solve these *Midnight Mysteries*.

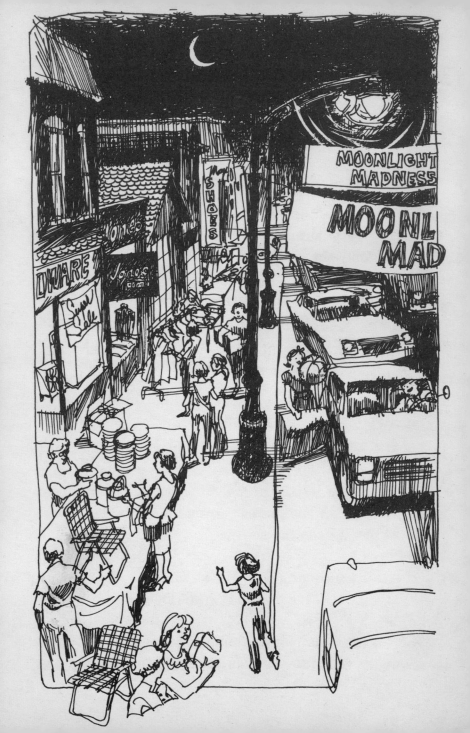

Moonlight Madness

Every summer, on a night near the end of August, the town of Claremont had a Moonlight Madness sale.

Along the main street, five blocks of shopkeepers set up tables on the sidewalk and wheeled out racks of clothes. Summer was over, and all the summer stock had to go. Sun-dresses, straw hats, sandals, camping equipment, beach balls, bathing suits, lemonade pitchers. The tables were stacked high.

The sale began at ten o'clock at night and lasted as long as the shopkeepers still had customers. It was called Moonlight Madness because all the prices were so low. Banners were strung across the street:

Crazy prices — We've lost our minds
MOONLIGHT MADNESS

Laurie Jamieson thought Moonlight Madness night was fun. It was exciting to be shopping along the sidewalks so late at night, long after dark. She liked the throngs of people, the overflowing tables, and the colorful racks of clothes. There was a holiday atmosphere in the crowded street lit by street lamps and lights from the shops.

Usually Laurie went to the sale with her mother. But this year Laurie had her driver's license, and Mrs. Jamieson said Laurie and her friend Marjory could go to the sale alone.

"I've been to a hundred Moonlight Madness nights," Mrs. Jamieson said. "I'm going to skip this one."

"A hundred?" Laurie teased. "I didn't know you were that old."

Mrs. Jamieson smiled. "Well, let's say a dozen. Anyway, I'm going to skip this one."

Laurie drove through the streets to Marjory's house cautiously. She hadn't had her driver's license very long, and she wanted to do everything just right. She felt very daring, out alone on the dark summer night. It was just a few minutes past ten when she pulled up in front of Marjory's house. Marjory had been watching for her, and before Laurie could honk the horn, Marjory came running down the front steps. She was just as excited as Laurie about going to the Moonlight Madness sale; she had money to spend tucked safely in the pocket of her jeans.

"Hi!" she greeted Laurie cheerfully. But as she slipped into the front seat beside Laurie she almost sat on a long cardboard box.

"Wait," Laurie said. "Let me get this out of your way. It's Mom's silver candlesticks. She's letting my Aunt Marian borrow them for a party tomorrow. I have to drop them off at Aunt Marian's house."

Laurie drove on, and Marjory sat holding the box with the candlesticks on her lap. Aunt Marian's house was soon in sight. A lamp shone in the living-room window.

"I'll take the candlesticks in," Marjory offered. So Laurie stayed in the car, feeling important with the gearshift in "Park" and the headlights shining on the asphalt paving of the street.

But Marjory came back, still carrying the box with the candlesticks.

She opened the car door and stuck in her head. "No one answered the doorbell."

Laurie was baffled for a moment. There was a light on in Aunt Marian's living room. Why didn't she answer the door?

But lots of people left a light on when they went out at night.

"She's probably already gone to the sale," Laurie decided.

"What about the candlesticks?" Marjory asked, as she got back into the car.

Laurie shrugged. "We can try on our way home. Or I can bring them over in the morning."

"Okay." Marjory swung the car door shut and twisted around to put the cardboard box on the back seat.

Then they were on their way.

Parking places along the streets were quickly filled on Moonlight Madness nights. So was the parking lot behind the supermarket. Laurie's mother had always found a place there. But when Laurie and Marjory arrived, every spot was taken.

Laurie left the supermarket lot and drove slowly along the main street. Shoppers had already gathered. The best bargains were already being snapped up. But there was no place to park.

Marjory looked through the car window anxiously. She wanted to get out and start exploring all the wonderful things for sale.

Laurie also wanted to join the people clustered around the tables and clothes' racks. But as her Dad always said, "You can't stick a car in your hip pocket. You've got to park it *somewhere*."

As they came toward the end of the blocks of stores, Marjory turned to Laurie. She didn't really want to suggest it, but she said, "Maybe Jake Thorp still has room."

"Maybe he does—" Laurie sounded reluctant. "But he's so mean-looking. I never liked him."

Jake Thorp had a small repair shop at the far

end of the main street. He didn't have anything to sell on Moonlight Madness night, but he opened the vacant lot beside his repair shop for a parking area. He sat in a sagging lawn chair at the corner of his lot and charged people $1.50 to park there.

"I don't like him either," Marjory agreed. "But let's try. We can't drive around forever."

The repair shop was just ahead. And there sat Jake Thorp as grand as a king in his old chair, pipe smoke drifting about his head, his hand ready for the next $1.50 to come along.

Which was Laurie's.

Jake Thorp had always frightened Laurie a bit. He was tall, and his face was whiskery and sly-looking. But there were some empty places near the back of his lot, and Laurie was glad to see them. Driving was fun, but enough was enough.

When the girls came back to Jake Thorp's lot it was nearly midnight. Their arms were filled with crinkly paper bags from the Moonlight Madness sale. Their faces were bright with smiles—which faded as Laurie unlocked the car and started to dump her packages onto the back seat.

"Marjory! The box is gone! The candlesticks—they're gone!"

"Gone? Oh, Laurie, are you sure?" Marjory shifted her packages and tried to see into the car.

"They're *gone,*" Laurie repeated.

6

"Look on the floor," Marjory said. "Maybe the box fell."

"How could it fall to the floor?" But Laurie looked there anyway. She groped about on the floor and under the car seat.

But there was nothing there.

"Marjory—they're gone!" Laurie's voice sank with dismay. She had wanted to do everything just right tonight, her first time to drive to a Moonlight Madness sale by herself. And now her mother's beautiful silver candlesticks were gone—stolen.

"But the car was locked." Marjory stood by helplessly, clutching her packages.

"People can get into locked cars," Laurie reminded her.

Marjory nodded unhappily. "Oh, Laurie, what will we do?"

Laurie didn't know what they could do. She stood staring bleakly at Marjory. She felt so miserable she wanted to cry. The Moonlight Madness night had been so much fun, and now everything was ruined.

"Maybe *he* took them," Marjory whispered. She motioned toward the front of the lot, where Jake Thorp sat on his worn-out chair.

"I bet he did," Laurie agreed eagerly. She had never trusted mean-looking Jake Thorp. He

probably lured people into his parking lot just so he could steal things out of their cars. He frightened her, but now she was more angry than frightened.

"I'm going to ask him," she declared, slamming the car door with a dreadful bang. "I'm going to go right up there and ask him."

"You are?" Marjory didn't want to go anywhere near Jake Thorp. But she couldn't let Laurie go alone. When they reached Jake, she stood behind Laurie, crushing her paper bags and wishing she was a thousand miles away.

Even though it was now midnight, the sidewalk sale was still bustling. Music blared from a loud-speaker. Banners fluttered in the summer breeze.

Laurie faced Jake Thorp boldly, but her heart was in her throat.

"Mr. Thorp, someone has stolen something from my car. When I came to park, I had a box of candlesticks on the back seat. And now they're gone."

"I'm not responsible for what's in these cars," Jake said gruffly. He squinted at Laurie through the smoke from his pipe.

"Well, you ought to be responsible." Laurie fumbled for words. "If people come here to park, their cars ought to be safe."

Jake Thorp was on his feet now. He looked tall

and mean. Marjory moved back another step behind Laurie.

"Maybe you know something about those candlesticks yourself." Laurie plunged on. "I don't think it's very nice to charge people for parking their cars, and then stealing things out of them."

"See here—" Jake Thorp's voice was raspy. "I don't know anything about your candlesticks. What would I want with an old pair of silver candlesticks?"

"You could sell them," she stammered. "They're valuable antiques."

"I never left this chair." Jake Thorp looked tough enough to chew nails, and he sounded like he meant what he said.

Laurie hesitated. Maybe she was wrong about Mr. Thorp. Maybe somebody else had stolen the candlesticks after all.

"Did you see anyone around in the lot?" she asked. "Anyone suspicious?"

Jake Thorp rubbed his bristly chin. "Yeah, come to think of it—a boy ran through here a little while ago. I hollered at him to get out of my lot."

Laurie thought this might be the answer. But what boy? How could she ever find him? The town was full of boys.

"Did you recognize him?" she asked hopefully, but Jake Thorp looked disgusted at such a question. "Naw, he was just a kid. You think I know every kid in town?"

"No, I guess not," Laurie answered lamely. She could hear a rustling sound behind her as Marjory shifted her packages. Jake Thorp was silent. In the street beyond, loud-speaker music played for the Moonlight Madness sale.

"Well, he had kind of dark hair," Jake said grudgingly.

"Dark hair?" Laurie felt discouraged. The town was full of boys with dark hair. "Can't you remember anything else?" she pleaded.

Jake Thorp shook his head. "Big kid, with dark hair. That's all I know. Ran off that way." He jerked a thumb toward the sidewalk sale and the bright banners that were strung across the street.

There didn't seem to be anything else to say. Laurie and Marjory walked back through the dark lot toward the car.

"How can the police ever find a boy with dark hair?" Laurie moaned. "That's no description. I'll never find Mom's candlesticks. It's hopeless."

"It's *not* hopeless," Marjory said. "We'll go to the police and tell them about the candlesticks, and we'll get them back."

Laurie looked at Marjory with surprise. "What do you mean?"

Marjory smiled over her armload of packages.

She felt a little nervous, but she was sure she was right.

"I know who took the candlesticks."

How did Marjory know who had stolen the candlesticks?

For the answer, turn to page 55.

No Escape

The television movie was drawing to an end. On the screen, lightning flashed and rain pounded at the windows of the gloomy old house where so many weird events had taken place. Thunder rumbled. Lightning flashed again. A clock began to strike—in a house where no clocks were allowed.

"The curse is fulfilled," the hero screamed.

With a final flash of lightning, the movie was over.

Jimmy and his sister Ruthie had watched every minute of it, wide-eyed at all the frightening twists in the story of *The House Without Clocks.*

On the television screen a commercial began. A white-haired woman with a smiling face was saying, *"I'm so glad you came. I've just made coffee. It's a new kind..."*

Ruthie turned off the set and shook her head wonderingly. "Imagine living in a house without clocks."

"Yeah," Jimmy agreed. "Hey, I read a story

once about a man who lived in a house without mirrors."

"That would be worse than no clocks." Ruthie looked stunned.

"Well, we don't live without clocks," their father said cheerfully. "And our clocks say it's time for you two to be in bed."

But even after Jimmy was in bed, he kept thinking about the television movie. The old house full of dark corners and endless winding stairways ...the hero in the cellar holding a flickering candle... a rat running across the floor...

It was hard to get to sleep after such a scary program. The last time Jimmy looked at the clock beside his bed, it was already past eleven thirty. And as he drifted off to sleep at last, he could hear a clock striking twelve. Through a misty darkness he could see the face of the clock rippling like a reflection under water. He could see the great brass pendulum swinging, glinting with light.

In his dream he stood in a large hallway. The clock towered above him, striking the hour of midnight with a slow, steady beat. A door opened, and a smiling, white-haired woman came toward Jimmy. *"I'm so glad you came,"* she said. Her face hovered close to his, as though it floated in the shadows with no body attached. Her eyes were two blank circles of light. *"I'm so glad you came...now follow me."*

Her face floated ahead of him along the hall. A hand beckoned in the shadows. Jimmy wanted to run away, but he kept following the floating face and the beckoning hand.

A door opened, and Jimmy stood looking into a room he seemed to know and yet not know. He heard the woman laugh softly. *"In this room, there are no mirrors."*

The room slid away and dissolved. The face and the beckoning hand led Jimmy along the hall to another room.

This time the voice was close to his ear, whispering, *"In this room, there are no clocks."*

Jimmy looked at the floating face. "Why aren't there any clocks?" he asked. He didn't like this house, with things missing from rooms. He felt that something dreadful was going to happen.

"No clocks...no clocks..." the voice echoed softly. The woman was still smiling, but Jimmy didn't like her smile anymore. "I have to go home," he said. It was so late. He could hear the clock in the hallway beyond, striking with a heavy, warning beat. "I have to go home," he said again. But the face floated up a stairway, and Jimmy followed.

The stairway went on and on and on. Turning and twisting, disappearing, returning. Then another door opened and the woman said, *"Here is the last room. You must find out for yourself what is missing. I won't tell you this time."* She began to

laugh again, but it wasn't a cheerful laugh. It was a wicked, mocking laugh. Jimmy had never heard a laugh so evil.

"You must find out what is missing." Jimmy felt himself pushed into the room. *"You must find out what I will not allow here."*

"You mean like mirrors or clocks?" Jimmy asked.

"Exactly!" The voice had a hollow, faraway sound.

Jimmy stared around the room. He could see his own reflection in a mirror on the wall. On a nearby table a clock was ticking. So it wasn't mirrors or clocks that were missing...but it could be *anything* ...how could he ever find out what was missing?

17

Behind him the woman with the wicked smile was slowly closing the door. In a moment Jimmy would be alone in the room. He turned and called after her, "It's not fair! How can I find what's not here?"

"*You'll find it,*" she promised with a last ghoulish laugh.

Then the door closed, and she was gone.

At breakfast the next morning, Jimmy told Ruthie about his dream. He remembered most of it. Some parts had faded in his memory, but he remembered the great clock, the floating face, and the last room.

Their father had already left for work, but their mother sat at the table and listened as Jimmy told his dream to Ruthie.

Jimmy wasn't afraid of the dream anymore, but as he told it, Ruthie shivered and said, "That sounds awful! Why didn't you just run away?"

Jimmy shrugged. "You know how dreams are. I didn't think of running away—at least not at first. I thought I had to stay in the room until I found out what was missing."

"But that would be impossible," Ruthie argued.

Jimmy buttered his toast. "Not really," he said calmly. "I found it."

"You did?" Ruthie looked at him with surprise. "How did you find it?"

"Because finally I gave up looking." Jimmy

smiled at Ruthie with a teasing expression.

"That doesn't make any sense." Ruthie twisted a strand of brown hair and frowned at Jimmy. "How can you find something when you give up looking?"

"Think about it." Jimmy took a bite of toast.

Ruthie turned to her mother. "What do *you* think, Mom?"

Her mother shook her head. "I'm just as lost as you are, Ruthie. But I have to get ready for work now. You'll have to figure out Jimmy's dream by yourself."

She left the table, and Ruthie turned back to Jimmy. "Tell me," she begged.

"You can figure it out if you just think," Jimmy insisted.

"What's to think about?"

"I said I only found it when I gave up," Jimmy reminded her. "What would I do if I gave up?"

"You'd try to run away," Ruthie said quickly.

"That's right." Jimmy had finished his toast. He buttered a second slice. Morning sunlight streamed across the kitchen. A geranium plant bloomed on the windowsill. It was a bright, cheerful room. Very different from the mysterious, shadow-filled rooms of his dream.

"Okay," Ruthie said. "You gave up and decided to get out of the room. What happened then?"

"Oh, I didn't get out of the room." Jimmy shook his head.

"Was the door locked?"

Jimmy ate his toast and thought about this for a moment. "I don't know," he said at last.

"But you found out what was missing in the room?"

"I sure did."

Ruthie tossed her head. "Oh, come on—I give up."

Do you give up?

For the answer, turn to page 55.

The Intruder

When Dorrie and her friend Ellen started out for the movie theater, snow was beginning to fall.

While they sat in the theater, eating popcorn and enjoying the movie, the snow outside grew heavier, covering the streets with a thick white blanket. When they came out of the theater, it was snowing hard. A strong wind had risen, whirling the snow and tugging at their coats.

"This is like a blizzard!" Dorrie laughed breathlessly as they struggled along.

The falling snow gave an eerie brightness to the street. The street lamps cast misty rings of swirling light.

It wasn't easy wading through the dense, wind-driven snow; but the two friends had only a couple of blocks to walk. Dorrie's small apartment building was across the street from the building where Ellen lived, and they parted at Dorrie's front entrance. Dorrie waited by her doorway until Ellen was across the street and turned to wave "good night." Now they were both safely home.

Dorrie went into the entry of her building, stamping snow from her boots. She had been living in the building, in apartment 2-B, for nearly a year. It was the first apartment she had ever had on her own.

It was fun, having her very own apartment. But she looked forward to moving to a better building, as soon as she could earn more money at her job. The building had six apartments. It was old and was not kept up as well as Dorrie would have liked. Her kitchen faucet dripped. Her refrigerator was making unpleasant, grating noises. She had mentioned both of these things to Mrs. Potter, the owner of the building. But so far Mrs. Potter had not sent anyone rushing up to fix the faucet or check the refrigerator.

And now, tonight, Dorrie saw that the light by the hallway stairs was out. The first-floor entrance hall was dimly lit, but the stairs rose ahead of her in almost total darkness.

"What next?" Dorrie muttered to herself.

Mrs. Potter lived in apartment 1-A, and Dorrie glanced at her door. But it was too late to disturb Mrs. Potter. At least Dorrie thought so. Mr. Benjamin, a fiery-tempered giant of a man who lived in the other first-floor apartment, wouldn't have hesitated. Dorrie could imagine him pounding on Mrs. Potter's door any hour of the day or night without a second thought. *Wake up, old woman—*

there's a light out! Then when Mrs. Potter eased open her door, blinking with sleep, he would stand towering over her, telling her for the hundredth time that the rents were too high, no wonder she had that third-floor apartment vacant so long now.

But Dorrie wasn't as bold as Mr. Benjamin. She wouldn't knock at Mrs. Potter's door at this late hour.

She cautiously made her way up the rickety stairs in the darkness, holding the banister. She was especially careful to step lightly on the third step, which she knew had a loose plank in it. At the top of the stairs, a light from the floor above cast shadows along the second-floor hall. Dorrie could barely make out her own door, and she was glad when she reached it.

But as she put her key in the lock, the door swung open by itself, creaking softly.

The sound of the opening door was the only sound in the deep silence of the apartment. The living room was faintly lit by the pale light of the snowy night beyond the windows. Then to her horror, Dorrie saw a slender figure standing in the living room, outlined against the center window. The figure rushed toward the door, knocking Dorrie aside with a rough motion.

Dorrie's purse fell to the floor. She was too frightened even to scream. Her heart was pounding as she heard the rapid thud of footsteps running

quickly down the stairs. A moment later she heard the front door open with a dull, sucking sound. Whoever had rushed down the stairs was gone now, out into the stormy night.

Afraid to move, Dorrie pressed back against the wall and tried to breathe. But she was so terrified, she felt she couldn't breathe. Her arm hurt where she had hit it against the wall, when the figure pushed past her.

The hallway was completely still now. Her eyes were growing used to the dark, and she could see the hall was empty. But was her apartment empty? Someone had come running out—was he the *only* intruder—or was someone else still in her apartment?

Dorrie's mind raced frantically. It wouldn't be safe to go into the apartment.

But she needed help...she should call the police...she should run away...

It was hard to think clearly.

The hallway was silent. Then, gradually, Dorrie became aware of a sound. It was only a low, muted sound, but she knew what it was. Mrs. McDougal across the hall in apartment 2-A was watching a late-night television show. Dorrie had often heard the soft murmur of Mrs. McDougal's television when she came home in the evenings. Mr. McDougal worked nights, and Mrs. McDougal watched television. Mrs. McDougal was awake and up—and there would be a telephone in her apartment.

Dorrie still didn't want to move, but she forced herself away from the wall. Her foot hit something, and as panic swept over her, she realized it was only her own purse. She had forgotten all about dropping it. She stooped and picked up the purse, and then she knocked at Mrs. McDougal's door.

Mrs. McDougal had her hair wrapped in curlers and her short, stout body wrapped in a faded blue bathrobe. She didn't mind turning off television for a real-life mystery.

Dorrie stayed in her apartment until the police car came.

Mrs. McDougal padded back and forth by the windows in her slippers, watching for the police and mumbling to herself about ruffians who broke into decent people's homes. When she saw the police car pull up in front of the building, she went into the dark hallway and leaned over the railing.

"Up here, up here," she called.

After the police officer made sure no one was in Dorrie's apartment, he asked Dorrie to come in and tell him what had happened. Mrs. McDougal came right along with Dorrie, hair curlers, bathrobe, and all. She didn't want to miss anything.

"What a mess," she anounced at once.

Dorrie was too shaken to say anything. She stood inside the doorway of her apartment and looked around at her small living room with dismay. The sofa cushions were on the floor, the drawers of her desk had been emptied out on the carpet. It was a distressing sight.

It was just as bad in the other rooms. In the kitchen, drawers had been yanked out. Cupboard doors hung open.

In the bedroom, dresser drawers had been dumped on the floor. The covers on the bed were torn off.

"It's my guess you won't find much missing," the officer said. "It looks to me like whoever was here was looking for money—or jewelry to sell, something like that."

"Jewelry?" Dorrie shook her head vaguely. "I don't have any jewelry. At least, not anything anybody would want—except maybe my opal ring—"

"Let's see if it's here," the police officer said.

"Where did you keep it?" Mrs. McDougal peered at Dorrie.

"I kept it in this drawer." Dorrie stared at the bedroom floor where the contents of a bedside table had been dumped. She knelt and poked around among the sprawl of things on the floor. The little green velvet box where she kept the ring was gone. The beautiful opal ring that had been a graduation present.

They went back to the living room, and the

officer kindly said, "Now, Miss, tell me exactly what happened." His presence was reassuring, but Dorrie still felt dazed.

"Sit down, dear," Mrs. McDougal said. "You're pale as a ghost."

Dorrie sank down on the edge of a chair and twisted her fingers nervously. She had been laughing on her way home from the movie. Her cheeks had been pink from the cold wind. Now she huddled on the chair white-faced and bewildered.

"I came home from the movies," she said helplessly. "And there was someone here."

"Go on, dear," Mrs. McDougal urged. She stood by the chair and patted Dorrie's hand.

"When I started to unlock the door, it wasn't locked. It just sort of swung open by itself."

Dorrie paused and looked at the officer. He motioned for her to go on.

"I could see someone standing by the window. Then he came running past me and knocked me against the wall."

"Did you recognize this person?" the police officer asked.

Dorrie shook her head. "It was so dark. He was just an outline at the window. I couldn't see his face."

"How about when he came running past you?"

Dorrie shook her head again. "I still didn't see his face. It was too dark in the hallway."

"But you must have gotten some general impression," he suggested. "A tall fellow? Short? Fat? Young? Old?"

Dorrie twisted her fingers and tried to remember.

"Young," she said, remembering how quickly the intruder had dashed past her. "And he wasn't very tall, about my height. Not fat—just average — oh, I don't know, it all happened so fast."

"Your height?" Mrs. McDougal pulled her bathrobe closer and nodded. "I bet it was that Barnes boy from upstairs. He's no good, been in lots of trouble."

The police officer agreed with this. He knew the troublemakers in the neighborhood, and Sammy Barnes was certainly one of them.

"But he didn't run upstairs," Dorrie said. She felt confused. Sammy Barnes and his mother lived in 3-B, right above Dorrie.

"He ran downstairs?" the officer asked.

"Yes, he ran downstairs," Dorrie said. "I heard the downstairs door."

"That doesn't prove anything," the officer said. "Sammy would be too smart to run upstairs to his own apartment if he was caught by surprise in here."

"I suppose so," Dorrie murmured.

She knew what Sammy Barnes looked like, and

he *was* just about her own height. But she hadn't seen the intruder's face. Sammy wasn't the only neighborhood boy who got into trouble. She didn't want to accuse the wrong person.

The police officer waited patiently. "Take your time, Miss. Think about everything again, and maybe you'll remember something else."

Dorrie tried to remember something else. But all she could remember was the eerie sound of the door creaking open and the sight of someone standing by the window, then rushing past her, knocking her against the wall, knocking her purse to the floor.

"Was there anything distinctive about this person?" the officer asked. "Could you tell how he was dressed? Was he wearing a coat? A hat?"

Mrs. McDougal glanced at the police officer admiringly. "That's right," she said. "If it was Sammy, he wouldn't need a coat or hat to break into an apartment right here in the building. Anybody from outside would be all bundled up on a cold, snowy night like this."

The officer and Mrs. McDougal looked at Dorrie hopefully. But she couldn't remember if the person who had come past her was wearing a coat or a hat.

"It all happened so fast," she said miserably.

The room was silent.

Dorrie's words hung in the silence. *It all happened so fast.*

And then, suddenly, Dorrie broke the silence.

"Maybe it *was* Sammy Barnes—yes, it must have been."

What made Dorrie decide it must have been Sammy Barnes?

For the answer, turn to page 56.

The Gang

The *Best Buy Grocery* was open every night until one o'clock.

Millie Bowen didn't like the idea much—especially when it was her turn to work late.

Business was slow in the late hours. Who came to buy frozen green beans at ten o'clock? Who suddenly needed a pound of butter at midnight?

Even the display "specials" set up at the front of the store to attract customers had an abandoned look late at night. At one time, the special had been sets of dishes. START YOUR CHINA COLLECTION. FREE DINNER PLATE WITH FIVE-DOLLAR PURCHASE. In early spring the china was gone, and the special was grass seed. LET YOUR LAWN GROW GREEN!

Millie had seen specials come and go. Snow shovels, Easter lilies, free dinner plates, grass seed, phonograph records. Now it was summer. The Fourth of July was coming up, and the special was picnic gear. Picnic baskets, paper plates, paper napkins, paper cups, thermos bottles. MAKE

YOUR PICNIC THE PERFECT PICNIC.

Millie sighed and looked at the clock. It was five minutes to twelve. At one o'clock she could go home. But one o'clock seemed a long way off.

The store was nearly deserted. The parking lot outside was filled only with the heat of the summer night. Beyond Millie's check-out counter, the aisles of the grocery store were lined with breakfast cereals, laundry soaps, jars of applesauce. A solitary late-night shopper pushed a cart along slowly. In one aisle, a stock boy was stamping prices on cans of tuna fish. Millie yawned wearily.

"Come on, Millie," Mr. Branigan teased as he came by her register. "It can't be that bad."

Mr. Branigan was the night manager. He

always had something cheerful to say. His smiling face was one of the bright spots in the dreary night hours.

"I missed some good TV tonight," Millie called back. Mr. Branigan walked on with a wave of his hand.

There was a display of transistor radios beside the picnic baskets and paper plates, and as Millie glanced toward it, a group of boys came into the store. They hovered around the radios. TAKE A RADIO ON YOUR PICNIC—$12.95—SPECIAL BUY.

They're up to no good, Millie thought to herself as she watched the boys. One of the boys was wearing a black leather jacket. Another boy wore a tight T-shirt with bright green letters across the front that read KISS ME, KID. A short, stocky boy wore a T-shirt that said I'M THE KING.

Millie didn't like the gang of boys. Even the last boy, who wore a baseball cap and a plain white T-shirt, didn't reassure her. They stood around the radios, clustered together as if they were trying to hide something.

Millie was glad Mr. Branigan was nearby. As the boys started to leave she called to him. "Mr. Branigan, those boys—"

Mr. Branigan came striding forward as the boys darted for the door.

"I think they took a radio," Millie said breathlessly.

Mr. Branigan began to run toward the door.

He had almost reached the boys as they went through the door. Each one ran in a different direction.

Mr. Branigan felt the hot blast of the early-July heat wave as he came out of the cool store. He saw the boys scattering.

But he knew which boy to grab. He knew which one was carrying the stolen radio.

How did Mr. Branigan know which boy had the radio?

For the answer, turn to page 56.

Midnight Mysteries

Usually, Dave Warner was in bed by ten o'clock. But there was going to be a math test at school the next day, and he wanted to study. He sat at the desk in his room. The lamp cast a circle of light on the pages of his math book.

He had lost track of the time. He didn't even realize his mother was coming along the hall until she stopped in the open doorway of his room.

"Hey, genius," she teased. "Do you know it's almost midnight?"

Dave pushed the book away and grinned. "All the numbers are beginning to look the same."

Mrs. Warner laughed. "Go to bed," she said. "Sleep tight."

And then the doorbell rang.

Dave and his mother stared at each other. The smile faded from Mrs. Warner's face. They were alone in the house—and the doorbell was ringing at an hour it had never rung before.

"Who can that be?" Mrs. Warner asked uneasily.

Dave certainly didn't know. It gave him a strange feeling to hear the doorbell ringing now, when it was nearly midnight.

"I'll get it," he said, pushing back the desk chair. His father had been dead for two years. Dave was the man of the family now.

His mother followed him along the hall. "Keep the chain on," she whispered behind him. "When you open the door, keep the chain on."

In the living room, the lamp Mrs. Warner kept lit all night burned dimly on a table near the windows. All the other lights were out. Who could be ringing the doorbell *now?*

"The chain—" Dave heard his mother say again.

There was a switch for the porch light by the door, and Dave flicked it on. Then he opened the door. It moved a few inches, and came to a stop against the chain. Through the small opening he saw a tall figure holding a flat, white cardboard box.

"Tony's Pizza," a voice said cheerfully.

Dave peered through the few inches of open door.

"What is it?" His mother was close behind him.

Dave looked at her with bewilderment. "It's a pizza."

"A pizza?" Mrs. Warner said in surprise.

Dave turned back to the door. "We didn't order

a pizza," he said to the delivery man standing there.

A sheet of paper was taped to the cardboard box, and the man looked down at it.

"This is 1004 Pine Street?"

"Yes, it is," Dave said. "But we didn't order a pizza."

"Close the door," Mrs. Warner whispered. It made her nervous, talking to strangers at this unlikely hour of the night.

The delivery man looked annoyed. "It's the right address," he insisted.

"I'm sorry." Dave shook his head again. "Really, we didn't order any pizza."

Through the small opening in the door Dave watched the tall figure go down the steps. A small van was parked at the curb, and the man drove off.

Dave closed the door and switched out the porch light. "I guess they got the address mixed up."

Mrs. Warner began to smile. "Somewhere somebody's waiting for a pizza, and it's not going to get there."

They laughed about it a little as they went back along the hallway to their bedrooms.

"Now you get to bed," Mrs. Warner said, "You've studied enough for tonight."

As Dave got ready for bed, he felt a bit anxious. Partly he was still worrying about the math test the next day. And partly he was remembering what had happened at school that afternoon.

There was a boy named Mike Corman who didn't know two times two was four. He was usually waiting for Dave at the classroom door, big and burly and full of questions. "What's the answer to number one?" he'd ask Dave. "What's the answer to number two?" His homework paper was always blank.

Dave had told him a few answers.

But the days went on, and Mike Corman was always there, waiting for Dave.

Once he had jerked Dave's notebook right out of his hand and thumbed through the pages looking for Dave's homework paper.

"Here we go!" he said when he found it. "Thanks, pal."

Dave lay awake thinking about Mike. Today when Mike wanted the math answers Dave had said, "Why don't you try to do a little homework yourself?"

It was the first time he had spoken like that to big Mike Corman.

He had held his notebook tight under his arm, so Mike couldn't grab it away. And then Mr. Fisher, the math teacher, came walking along. Mike backed off, holding up his hands in surrender. "Just kidding, Dave," he said.

But Dave knew Mike wasn't kidding.

Homework papers were handed in. Mike didn't have one. Halfway through class, Dave saw Mike glaring at him across the aisle.

He dreaded seeing Mike at school tomorrow.

The pizza delivery had amused Dave's mother. At least they had still been up when the delivery man came. But the next night both Dave and his mother were sound asleep when a taxi pulled up in front of their house. The driver began honking the horn.

By and by the cab driver stomped up the walk and rang the bell.

It was just like the pizza delivery. A mistake. But Mrs. Warner was frightened to have been awakened like this, and Dave couldn't get to sleep afterwards.

They hadn't ordered a pizza. They hadn't called for a cab. Why were these people coming to their house at midnight?

Next came the phone calls.

Every night for three nights, exactly at midnight, the phone rang. It was startling to hear the shrill ringing through the silent house. Something bad must have happened if somebody was calling at midnight.

But there was never anyone on the phone. At least, whoever was on the other end of the line never spoke.

After a moment or so, the receiver was replaced

by the caller.

By the third night, Dave found himself lying awake, waiting for the call.

Mrs. Warner was puzzled and frightened.

"Who could be calling like that?" she always said as she came back along the hall from the phone. Dave, standing in the doorway of his room, could only shake his head.

On Monday morning Mr. Fisher handed back the graded math tests. He went up and down the aisles, stern and silent, passing out the papers himself. The only student he spoke to was Mike Corman. Dave heard him say to Mike, "You've got to do better."

As Mr. Fisher moved on, Mike crumpled his paper into a ball and tossed it across the room. Several kids snickered, but when Mr. Fisher turned around there was nothing to see. Mike's failing test paper rolled into a corner.

The next morning was dark and gloomy. It was going to rain. In the small kitchen of the Warner house, a weather forecast was on the radio.

Sixty percent chance of rain this morning, increasing to eighty percent by afternoon...

As Dave came into the kitchen, Mrs. Warner switched off the radio. She had other things on her mind besides weather forecasts. She took a carton of eggs from the refrigerator. Dave thought she looked worried and tired. He felt tired himself. It was hard to get back to sleep after late-night arrivals at the door and midnight phone calls. Last night had been the fourth call.

"Dave, I think someone is playing a mean joke on us," Mrs. Warner said as she took eggs from the carton. "Can you think of anybody who would do such a thing? Make phone calls, send the cab, the pizza? It's too much to be just a coincidence."

Dave thought about Mike Corman. Mike was the only one he could think of who might be angry enough to cause all this trouble.

"Well," Dave began slowly, "There's a guy at school who's kind of mad at me."

Mrs. Warner forgot the eggs and came to sit at the table beside Dave. "Who?"

"Just one of the guys." Dave shrugged. "His name's Mike. I used to give him homework answers in math, and then one day I told him to do his own homework."

"Oh," Mrs. Warner looked disappointed. "Homework papers. I don't think that's reason enough to waken people late at night and frighten them like this."

She went back to the stove and began to fry eggs for breakfast. Dave watched her, thinking maybe she was wrong. Homework papers, tests, cross teachers, failing grades—they were a lot more important than she realized. School was the biggest thing in your life, when you had to go every day.

The more Dave thought about it, the more he thought Mike Corman was the one who had sent the pizza and the cab, and had made the phone calls. It would be Mike's idea of a good way to get even. Mike knew Dave and his mother lived alone. If Dave's father was still alive, Dave bet Mike wouldn't dare try such stuff.

Dave walked to school, thinking about Mike Corman all the while. Should he ask him about the phone calls, the cab, the pizza? What could he say? *Hey, did you send a pizza to my house last Thursday night?* That sounded dumb. Anyway, Mike would say he didn't send the pizza, or do any of the other things. Then what? Dave didn't have any real proof—or any way of stopping Mike's pranks.

Math was Dave's third class. The desk across the aisle was empty. Maybe Mike was absent, and Dave wouldn't have to decide whether to talk to him or not. It was a relief.

But at the last moment, as the bell rang, Mike slumped into the seat across the aisle. He looked as big and mean as ever.

It's too late now, Dave thought. The class was starting. It was too late to talk to Mike. And Dave was just as glad it had worked out that way.

"Turn to page 83," Mr. Fisher announced from his desk at the front of the room.

There was a noisy rustling of pages in math books. Outside, the first drops of rain began to fall. The weather report had been right.

The rain went on all day. At dinner that evening, Dave's mother picked at her food. "I wonder what will happen tonight," she said.

Dave wondered too. He was in bed by ten. The alarm clock, set for seven, ticked on the table by his bed. His door was closed. But the house was small, and he could hear the muffled voice of the ten o'clock newscaster on the television in the living room.

At first he lay alert, waiting. But he was short on sleep from the past nights, and soon he fell asleep.

He was wakened by a violent, pounding noise.

Bang.

Bang.

Bang.

Dave had no idea what time it was or how long he had been asleep. He was too groggy at first to even know what he was hearing. It was just a terrible racket.

Bang.

Bang.

Bang.

Just as he finally realized it was someone

pounding on the front door, a piercing, brilliant light crossed his windows.

In the dark of his bedroom, this harsh light flashed back and forth.

Dave struggled up from bed and went to the windows. He was half-asleep, frightened and bewildered. Outside, a police car was ranging a spotlight across the house—into Dave's room, then along the house to other rooms.

Behind the police car was another squad car, a circle of light flashing on its roof.

Bang.

Bang.

Bang.

The pounding on the door went on. The spotlight swept the house. It was all unreal, like a dream. But it wasn't a dream.

"Dave—" His mother was at the door of his room.

"It's the police," Dave answered through the darkness. His mother stood silhouetted in the light from the hall.

The pounding noise echoed through the house insistently, and together they went toward the door. "What's happening?" Mrs. Warner murmured with distress.

She turned on the porch light as she opened the door. Two uniformed police officers stood on the porch.

"What is it?" Mrs. Warner stammered.

"You reported a prowler here?"

"A prowler?" Mrs. Warner didn't understand.

"Someone called from this house and said there was a prowler on the back porch."

Dave stood close to his mother. In the street outside, a passing car had stopped to see what was going on. Across the street, lights went on in several houses. The whole neighborhood was awake—wondering what police cars were doing at the Warner house at midnight.

"I didn't call you," Mrs. Warner said. She clutched her bathrobe around her anxiously. "We were asleep."

"Someone called and gave this address," the officer said.

"No—it wasn't me." Mrs. Warner's voice was trembling. It had upset her to be wakened by the banging at the door, spotlights playing across the house.

"Everything's all right here?" the officer asked. Behind him the other officer waited. The spotlight had been turned off, but the rotating, flashing lights continued on the squad cars in front of the house.

Another passing car had stopped to see what was going on.

The lights glowed in the houses across the street.

"Yes, everything's all right here," Mrs. Warner said. "I don't understand."

"Probably a prankster, ma'am. It happens. Sorry to upset you."

Dave watched as the officer and his partner went down the steps and back to the squad cars at the curb.

It was the worst thing that had happened.

It took Dave and his mother a long time to get to sleep when they went back to bed.

The last time Dave looked at his clock it was nearly three. He would be awfully tired in the morning. He wouldn't do very well in classes the next day...in math class. Maybe that was what Mike had in mind.

If it was Mike.

Now Dave was angry enough to talk to Mike.

The pizza had been funny. But things had gone a long way beyond that.

He knew where Mike's locker was, and he waited for him before classes began the next morning.

Mike came shuffling along with one of his buddies. He slowed down, then stopped, lifting his eyebrows with surprise to see Dave Warner standing by his locker.

"What's up?" Mike's voice was cautious.

Dave wished he could talk to Mike alone. But Mike's buddy was there. He didn't have any choice.

"What's going on?" Mike asked again.

Dave took a deep breath.

"I don't suppose you know anything about the police being at my house last night?"

Mike spread his hands. "The police? How would I know anything about that?"

"Or the phone calls, the pizza, the cab?" Dave tried to keep his voice steady.

Mike's pal looked at Dave curiously. "What's he talking about, Mike?"

Kids streamed by in the hallway on their way to classes.

"How do I know what he's talking about?" Mike turned to his friend with a careless grin.

"I'm talking about phone calls to my

house—the police coming—and you'd better stop it." Dave tried to speak firmly, but his palms were sweaty, his heart beat fast.

"Aw, come on. You think I did those things?" Mike shook his head with disgust. "I'm not even up that late. You got the wrong guy."

"The police came to your house?" Mike's friend wanted to know all the details. "What happened then?"

"Nothing," Dave said grimly. "We told them it was a mistake."

"Why did they come?"

Dave looked at Mike's pal. "They came because Mike called them and said he was calling from my house to report a prowler."

"You're crazy!" Mike hooted with laughter.

But Dave stood his ground.

"You did it, Mike. The pizza, the cab, the phone calls, everything."

Dave felt sure of himself. He felt on top. Mike couldn't scare him anymore.

He took another deep breath.

"And stop it, Mike. Or I'll be the next one to call the police."

How did Dave know for sure that it was Mike who was playing the tricks?

For the answer, turn to page 56.

Moonlight Madness

Finding a boy by using the vague description that he was a "big kid, with dark hair" would have been difficult—if not impossible.

But Marjory knew the police wouldn't have to look for any boy at all. She knew Jake Thorp had made up the story about a boy running through his lot.

Jake had asked: "What would I want with an old pair of *silver* candlesticks?"

Laurie had not said the candlesticks were silver. She had only said a pair of candlesticks was missing from her car.

Candlesticks can be made of many materials—brass, copper, wood, glass, or pewter. But Jake Thorp knew they were *silver* because he had seen them. He had stolen them out of Laurie's car.

The police found the candlesticks hidden on a shelf in Jake Thorp's repair shop.

No Escape

When Jimmy gave up looking, he ran toward the door—and when he reached it, he found what was not allowed in the room.

A small but very necessary thing.

A doorknob.

The door was a smooth surface of wood with no inside knob, no way to open it. Jimmy had discovered what was missing—and at the same time, he had discovered he was in a room from which there was no escape.

He was glad to wake up and realize he had been dreaming!

The Intruder

Dorrie hadn't been able to see the intruder very well. But she had heard him.

He had heard his footsteps racing down the stairs.

The dark stairs.

Dorrie had climbed the stairs cautiously, holding the railing because it was too dark to see the stairs. She had stepped lightly on the third step, which was broken. Only someone who knew the stairs well could have run down them so swiftly in the dark. Only someone who lived in the building would have known about the broken step. And Dorrie's description of a slender young man her own height ruled out everyone in the building except Sammy Barnes.

The police found Sammy at his usual late-night hangout, a coffee shop in the neighborhood. He denied being in Dorrie's apartment, but her opal ring was found in his pocket.

The Gang

It was a hot summer night. Three of the boys were wearing thin T-shirts. Only the boy wearing a jacket could hide something as big as a radio.

The boy had worn the leather jacket on such a hot night for just that reason, to conceal the radio.

Midnight Mysteries

All the events had occurred late at night. At midnight or close to midnight.

But Dave hadn't said what time they happened. And Mike hadn't asked.

From what Dave had said, no one could have known when

the pizza, the cab, the phone calls, and the police cars came.

But Mike said: *"I'm not even up that late."*

This gave Dave the clue that Mike knew the things had happened late at night.

And Mike wouldn't have known that unless he was the one who was responsible.